THE MYSTERIOUS MISSING BOOK

Written by REBECCA RUBIN SELIGSON
Illustrated by BRIGID MALLOY

Published by Rebecca Rubin Seligson - Wheellustrated Tales

Text Copyright 2021 TXu 2-273-551 by Rebecca Rubin
Illustration Copyright 2022 Belonging to Brigid Malloy Illustrations

Layout & Design by Travis D. Peterson at Launch Mission Creative
Author head shot photo: Yehonathan Elozory Photography

Published 2022

ISBN: 979-8-9869266-4-3 (paperback)
ISBN: 979-8-9869266-1-2 (hardcover)
ISBN: 979-8-9869266-2-9 (audiobook)
ISBN: 979-8-9869266-3-6 (e-book)

www.wheellustratedtales.com
www.brigidmalloy.com
www.launchmissioncreative.com

To Ezri, Noa, Kayla, & Eitan:

"Reach for your own words, tell the world who
you are, and how you will make it better."
-PETER H. REYNOLDS

LOVE, IMMA/REBECCA

"For the superheroes who don't always wear capes."

-BRIGID

"Be bold; be brave; let you be you...
and let's help others, too!"

-TRAVIS

I bet you have never met a superhero in real life.

My real name is Zee, but I'm really a superhero.

My hero name is INCREDI-WHEELS. I have an awesome cape, mask and costume, just like all the other superheroes!

I also have a cool utility bag, that has lots of tools to help on super-missions.

My little sister is also a superhero – she's my sidekick.

Her real name is Nina but her superhero name is

Super Sidekick Sister, or **"TRIPLE S"** for short.

We both have incredibly cool superpowers – I can zoom at super speed and she can climb just about anything!

We work together and make a great team to help
however we can. That's our job as superheroes -

WE ARE SUPER HELPERS!

One time, Nina and I were playing catch in the park, when suddenly, we heard someone yelling,

"HEY! WAIT! THAT'S MINE! GIVE IT BACK!"

That sounded like the words of someone who needed help!

It was our friend, Zoey.

We dashed over to see what happened.

"I was just over here on the bench, reading my book, when suddenly, I felt something big and furry walk past my legs. I heard a growl and then something snatched my book! How am I going to find it in this huge park all by myself?"

"That sounds so frustrating! Seems like a job for some super-helpers! Would you like us to help find your book? The park might be too big for one person to search alone, but if we can combine our superpowers, we can surely find it."

"Please!" Zoey said eagerly.

Incredi-Wheels and Triple S to the rescue!

Nothing gets in our way to help save the day!

And guess what - not only do Nina and I have superpowers, we helped Zoey discover her own superpower! "That's not JUST a cane – you can use it to help feel around for your book – like a super searching stick!"

We all worked together to come up with a plan. Each of us had a job to do and we used our special superpowers to make sure no stone was left unturned in the hunt for the missing book.

Zoey felt around the area
with the benches to check
if her book was there.

I sped around the playground, looking around
the slides, swings, and jungle gym. My utility
bag had my binoculars at the ready so I could
search far and wide for Zoey's book.

Triple S climbed up all the trees to get a birds-eye view of the park. Could she really spot the furry growler and the missing book from all the way up there?

"Over here!" yelled Triple S. "I see the book! And guess what else I see - a cat sitting up on that branch! The cat must have grabbed it from Zoey and climbed up with it."

"It's too far for me to reach, but I can knock it down with a branch! Incredi-Wheels, come catch it!"

I caught Zoey's book with one hand and Triple S climbed back down from the tree.

"Thank you, super helpers," Zoey said gratefully. "You were here for me when I needed you most. If it weren't for you, there's no way I would have been able to search the whole park by myself."